Jolteon

Flareon

Glaceon

Vaporeon

EEVEE

Espeon

Umbreon

Leafeon

Sylveon

Popplio → Brionne → Primarina

...ten → Torracat → Incineroar

D0012885

Rowlet → Dartrix → Decidueye

TOO CUTE

Some Pokémon are not quite ready to train, although they can have a Trainer. These tender, tiny Pokémon pals might look completely sweet, but don't test them. Although they may be little, they have a few skills to help them make their way in the world, and they can take care of themselves. But Trainers who care for them find these Pokémon need extra TLC until they are ready to evolve.

Some Pokémon with These Forms:

- Bonsly
- Mime Jr.
- Smoochum
- Togepi

By Simcha Whitehill

Published by Scholastic Inc., *Publishers since 1920.* SCHOLASTIC and associated logos are trademarks and/or registered trademarks of Scholastic Inc.

Based on *Pokémon: Evolution Manual* published in 2020 by Scholastic Inc.

Format and lenticular sticker development by Red Bird Publishing UK. Production by Red Bird Publishing UK.

The publisher does not have any control over and does not assume any responsibility for author or third-party websites or their content.

This book is a work of fiction. Names, characters, places, and incidents are either the product of the author's imagination or are used fictitiously, and any resemblance to actual persons, living or dead, business establishments, events, or locales is entirely coincidental.

ISBN 978-1-338-87139-5

10 9 8 7 6 5 4 3 2 1   23 24 25 26 27

Printed in China
First printing 2023

Book design by Cheung Tai

WHAT IS POKÉMON EVOLUTION?

Just as humans grow bigger and stronger, so too can many Pokémon. This important and mysterious process is called Pokémon Evolution. With proper nutrition and a dedication to training, a caring Pokémon Trainer can help their Pokémon pal evolve. But there is no single or obvious way to make something as magical as a Pokémon Evolution happen.

Some Pokémon can evolve once. Some Pokémon can evolve twice. Some Pokémon can Mega Evolve. Some Pokémon do not have a known Evolution. And some Pokémon do not want to evolve.

Inside this book, you will find important details and fun facts straight from the authorities on Pokémon. If you are interested in learning all you can about Pokémon Evolution, then all you need to do is read on!

HOW TO KNOW WHEN YOUR POKÉMON IS EVOLVING

When Pokémon grow up, they *glow* up! Typically, when a Pokémon is about to evolve, it is bathed in a bright glow. Inside this light, the Pokémon transforms. When the change is complete, the glow disappears, revealing the Pokémon in its new Evolution. It is quite a shining sight to see! Often, the Evolution will be bigger and stronger. The Pokémon will now have new abilities and possibly even be a new type.

EVOLUTION EXPERTS

Professor Rowan

The Sinnoh region's Professor Rowan is a renowned researcher. At his lab outside of Sandgem Town, he focuses his studies on Pokémon Evolution and habits. Rowan appreciates the unique personality of each Pokémon. To help nourish the bonds between a Pokémon and their Trainer, he hosts the Pokémon Summer Academy at Mt. Coronet. But he is a man of serious study, so you won't see him playing around.

Professor Birch

If you're looking for Professor Birch, you'll have to look all over the Hoenn region. This laid-back Pokémon researcher is rarely at his lab in Littleroot Town. Birch likes to get his hands dirty out in the field. He focuses his studies on the habits of wild Pokémon. Professor Birch is especially interested in examining unique evolutionary chains like Clamperl's.

Professor Juniper

You can find Professor Juniper in the Unova region, working at her lab in Nuvema Town or at her mobile lab near Chargestone Cave. The young professor has already made quite a name for herself through her technological advancements. Although the focus of her research is Pokémon origins, Professor Juniper created the Pokémon Trading Device, a computer that can successfully trade and evolve certain Pokémon during a battle. In fact, Professor Juniper traded her Pokémon Karrablast with Bianca's Shelmet, and using her Pokémon Trading Device, both Pokémon evolved in a flash! Professor Juniper was then paired with Accelgor and Bianca with Escavalier.

Professor Sycamore

From his lab in Lumiose City in the Kalos region, Professor Sycamore studies a temporary—but extremely powerful—form of Evolution: Mega Evolution. He is the leading expert on the subject and has even helped his best friend, Garchomp, Mega Evolve. In fact, Professor Sycamore cared for Garchomp since it was a little Gible, so they have been through multiple Evolutions together. Professor Sycamore's lab also has a huge Pokémon habitat on-site.

Professor Westwood V

Stationed on Seafoam Island, Professor Westwood is perhaps best known for programming the Pokédex. However, he is also fascinated by the evolutionary relationship between Slowpoke and Shellder. Professor Westwood comes from a long line of Pokémon researchers: He is the fifth Professor Westwood to make contributions to Pokémon science.

Hal

A researcher at the Izabe Island Academy, Hal is obsessed with an awesome way Trapinch evolve into Vibrava. As a child, he accidentally fell into the local Trapinch Underground Labyrinth, where he witnessed a group of Trapinch evolve together. It was so amazing, he couldn't wait to share his discovery. There was only one problem: No one believed him. So Hal studied hard and devoted his career to finding a way to prove and share his knowledge.

ADVANTAGES OF EVOLUTION

Trainers often hope to help their Pokémon evolve for a few key reasons.

GAIN SKILLS

When a Pokémon evolves, its new form possesses different physical characteristics and even the chance to learn different moves.

Even off the battlefield, Evolutions can be impressive. For example, when a Team Rocket mecha caught fire, Sliggoo evolved into Goodra so it could use a powerful Rain Dance to extinguish the flames.

When Swadloon evolved into Leavanny, it was able to make clothing using its sticky string and leaves. And after Burmy evolved into Mothim, it could smell the precious Enchanted Honey at the Amber Castle.

GAIN SIZE

In the majority of Evolutions, Pokémon grow larger. Swinub is a mere one foot four and a little over fourteen pounds. But when it evolves into Piloswine, it gains two feet, three inches, and roughly 109 pounds. Then, when it evolves again into Mamoswine, it shoots up to eight foot two and weighs in at a whopping 641.5 pounds!

That kind of size can be an impressive advantage in battle, but sometimes it can be quite a surprise. Once, when six-foot-seven Wailmer evolved into the over-forty-seven-foot Wailord while battling Swampert, it became too big to pass under the Canalave City harbor drawbridge—so Ash and Pokémon pals stepped in to help open the bridge for it.

GAIN STRENGTH

With size can come strength in many forms. A Pokémon might be able to lift heavier objects or even endure more attacks. Strength is quite an advantage in so many powerful ways. During battle, Slakoth was able to evolve into Vigoroth and thus become immune to its opponent Snorlax's fierce Yawn.

EVOLUTIONS DON'T ALWAYS WIN

While it might seem like an Evolution would always have the upper hand, it is wrong to assume that it is guaranteed to win in a battle against one of its earlier forms. So much of a battle outcome relies on a clever strategy and finding a Pokémon's true advantage. And sometimes, a Pokémon's power might just be that it is in its earlier form.

During a battle with Honchkrow, Turtwig was poised to win the battle because it was able to dodge moves quickly. But when it evolved mid-match into Grotle, it lost its speed and eventually the round.

On the other hand, Ash's pal Pikachu has defeated not one but two Raichu in fierce battles! And Dawn and Piplup won a contest battle against Kenny and Prinplup. A battle outcome is not decided by stats, but by the partnership of a Pokémon and its Trainer!

WHEN DO POKÉMON EVOLVE?

Pokémon can evolve in different ways, for different reasons, at all different times, and in many different places. While Evolution typically comes as a surprise to both the Trainer and the Pokémon, there are a couple more likely moments it may happen.

DURING BATTLE

Arguably the most common time Pokémon evolve is in the heat of battle. A Pokémon or Trainer might even want to battle for the sole purpose of helping the Pokémon evolve. When Bagon wanted to evolve, it asked Ash and Pikachu for a battle.

Sometimes not only one Pokémon evolves during a battle, but two! When Ash and his pal Treecko teamed up for a battle with Guy and a howling Loudred, both Pokémon evolved mid-match. Treecko became Grovyle, Loudred became an even louder Exploud.

The more heated the battle, the more likely an Evolution will occur. During big competitions, contests, matchups with heroes, and even battles with enemies, there could be that extra spark to start a Pokémon Evolution. Every time Ash and his rival Paul face off, the match is explosive! During the PokéRinger competition, Ash and his Pokémon Staravia were locked in an intense battle with Paul and Honchkrow. As Honchkrow looked like it was about to swoop in and serve the final blow with Sky Attack, Staravia evolved into speedy Staraptor, then grabbed the winning ring and sent it to the goal, sealing a victory!

WITH THE HELP OF EVOLUTION STONES

There is a way a Trainer can help a Pokémon pal evolve in an instant. It's hard to the touch and can be very hard to find: a Pokémon Evolution Stone.

There are many types of Evolution Stones. To help a Pokémon evolve, the correct one for its species must be used. For example, Pikachu can become Raichu with the aid of a Thunder Stone. Lombre evolved into Ludicolo with the help of a Water Stone. Skitty became Delcatty with a Moon Stone.

SOME HOT SPOTS FOR FINDING EVOLUTION STONES

In the Kanto region, under the peak of purple Evolution Mountain, sits a small village called Stone Town. Many Pokémon Trainers flock there in the hopes of finding Evolution Stones. The famous Eevee brothers have been known to host garden parties in Stone Town, and Trainers come together to help their Pokémon evolve with Evolution Stones.

In the Hoenn region, there is the great Granite Cave that many Aron call home. Steven Stone, a man on a mission for Evolution Stones, was also able to find the magnificent Fire Stone there.

At the foot of the mountains in Kalos is Geosenge Town, a city known for stores filled with important stones.

POKÉMON WHO EVOLVE TOGETHER

Some Pokémon band together to evolve. This unique experience is not common, and humans rarely get the chance to see it firsthand.

Bulbasaur

In a hidden valley, far from any human eyes, is a Mysterious Garden, where an incredible ceremony happens. According to legend, when the planets are in a specific position and the moon is in the correct phase, dozens of Bulbasaur and their blinking bulbs meet in this sacred spot in the middle of the night. Together, they gather beneath a massive tree. Suddenly, a bright light bursts from the tree, and a very large, important Venusaur appears. The Venusaur calls out to all the Bulbasaur, who reply in unison. Then, one by one, each Bulbasaur evolves into Ivysaur. And as the newly evolved Pokémon make their way back home, the Mysterious Garden disappears into thin air!

Morelull

The woods of Alola are filled with a wide variety of plant and Pokémon life. But humans must be on high alert for a tiny Pokémon—Morelull. The eight-inch-tall Pokémon shoots sparkling spores that will send anyone who sees it into dreamland. Then, while they're asleep, Morelull will drain their energy! But Morelull is perhaps less well known for the incredible light it can shine. When a group of Morelull gather at a special tree tucked away in the forest, the whole area glows! The Morelull's glow grows as they evolve into Shiinotic. And with their energy combined, the bare tree instantly blooms with spectacular red flowers!

Trapinch

On Izabe Island in the Hoenn region, there is a unique underground Pokémon habitat built by Trapinch. These desert-dwelling Pokémon love to dig in the sand, and they have built a series of tunnels into a maze that leads to a large, secret lake. There, groups of Trapinch gather at the banks of the lake and together evolve into Vibrava.

NOT ALL POKEMON WANT TO EVOLVE

Some Pokémon can't wait to evolve, and some never want to. For Pokémon, choosing to evolve is very personal. No matter what form or species, it is a big change and a big decision—and it's truly up to the Pokémon itself. When a Pokémon makes the choice not to evolve, it is sometimes a surprise to their Trainer, but a good Trainer will always support their Pokémon's decision.

EVERSTONES

An Everstone is a speckled gray stone that might look like just any old rock. But if it has these markings, it possesses a precious power. For a Pokémon that does not want to evolve, an Everstone makes the perfect gift, because it ensures Evolution won't happen.

As research continues on Everstones, they have been found to have an added effect. When Rowlet accidentally swallowed one and tried to spit it out, it learned Seed Bomb.

PROUD TO BE PIPLUP

When Dawn's first partner Pokémon Piplup was glowing, it seemed like it was going to evolve. But the light soon disappeared, leaving behind a very tired Piplup—it had been using Bide to block itself from evolving. When Dawn tried to talk to her Pokémon pal about evolving, it fled into the forest. Dawn followed Piplup, but they ended up surrounded by Ariados, and the two battled the Long Leg Pokémon together—until a Team Rocket robot arrived on the scene and captured Piplup.

Dawn crawled into the robot to fight for her Pokémon pal, and since Piplup was still small—and not a larger Evolution—it was able to crawl through a duct to back up its Trainer. Then it used Whirlpool to destroy the robot. Suddenly, it all clicked for Dawn—Piplup wanted to stay Piplup because it knew it can help protect Dawn as it was, with no Evolution necessary.

Touched, Dawn promised to always be Piplup's partner. Thanks to the local Nurse Joy, Dawn got an Everstone to help Piplup remain its wonderful self, no Bide necessary.

PIKACHU FOREVER

At first, when Pikachu faced Lt. Surge, the Gym Leader of Vermillion City and his supercharged Raichu, it lost the match. Nurse Joy offered Ash a Thunder Stone to help Pikachu evolve so that the rematch would be Raichu vs. Raichu—a more level playing field. But Pikachu ultimately decided to stay the Pikachu we know and love today. And it even defeated Raichu during the fierce rematch by being itself to the max!

Later, Pikachu faced Raichu again in battle and was defeated. While resting up at the Pokémon Center after the match, Ash considered using the Thunder Stone he has been carrying since Vermillion City. Before he could discuss it with Pikachu, though, Team Rocket stole the precious Thunder Stone! But Pikachu trained hard, and in its rematch with Sho and Raichu, Pikachu sealed a victory against its Evolution. Since then, it hasn't had a second thought about being anything but Pikachu!

PLACES AND SPACES SPECIAL TO EVOLUTION

The A-B-C Islands

These Islands are famous for helping Clamperl evolve in their caves. Professor Birch's research on the islands helped him discover what causes their branched Evolution: With the addition of pink Deepseascale found on Island B, Clamperl evolves into Huntail. With the help of Deepseatooth found on Island C, Clamperl evolves into Gorebyss.

Trapinch Underground Labyrinth

Hidden beneath a desert in the Hoenn region lies a secret labyrinth. Running through this maze is a tunnel that leads to a terrific lake where Trapinch gather to evolve into Vibrava.

The Mysterious Garden

No one knows the secret location of the place where Bulbasaur evolve into Ivysaur. It lies somewhere in the Kanto region, but it's not just a place—it's also a time. When the planets and moon align, the giant tree appears in the valley and summons the Bulbasaur.

The Altar of the Sunne

At the Altar of the Sunne, with the proper ritual from all four Island Guardians of Alola—Tapu Lele, Tapu Bulu, Tapu Fini, and Tapu Koko—a special Cosmoem nicknamed Nebby can evolve into the Legendary Pokémon Solgaleo and open the Wormhole to the world of the Ultra Beasts.

Some Pokémon might evolve into different forms or even different Pokémon. For example, depending on the time of day that Rockruff evolves into Lycanroc, it can become Lycanroc Midday Form or Lycanroc Midnight Form. Whether permanent, or a temporary Mega Evolution during battle, this type of Evolution with options is called branched Evolution.

SLOWPOKE AND SHELLDER

One Pokémon with a very interesting branched Evolution is Slowpoke. Slowpoke cannot evolve without Shellder, a partnership that benefits both of them. They are at their best when they experience this friendship and live together in harmony.

If Shellder bites Slowpoke's tail, it will evolve into Slowbro. But Shellder will also experience a change: Its shell will go from being hinged to being a solid spiral, and as it remains on Slowbro's tail, its balance improves and it can stand tall. Plus, with its hands free, it can deliver tough moves like Mega Punch. Shellder is also happy to hang on, because Slowbro can take it traveling on land.

While the vast majority of Slowpoke and Shellder join forces to become Slowbro, there is a chance this duo can also evolve into an important Pokémon leader. If Shellder manages to latch atop Slowpoke's head, it will evolve into the regal Slowking, and Shellder will become a bejeweled crown. It is no wonder the wise Slowking is called the Royal Pokémon.

While Slowpoke and Slowbro are typically not very intelligent, Slowking is considered to be a brilliant problem-solver, prepared to take on the world's toughest issues. But it is said that if the Shellder on its head ever falls off, it will forget everything!

THE EMOTIONS OF EVOLUTION

Evolution doesn't just bring about physical change—it can also involve an emotional change. There are many emotions that can cause an impact around a Pokémon Evolution.

So Lonely

Pokémon can feel alone and might even be cast out of their group once they evolve. After becoming Octillery, the Jet Pokémon was rejected by its friends—a group of its earlier form, Remoraid. It felt so sad and alone, it struggled to show its strength, and its Trainer feared they wouldn't make it to the Whirl Cup.

Anger

Many Pokémon feel full of anger after they evolve. Unsure of how to express themselves in their new body, it is not unusual for them to fly into a rage. Trainers, consider yourselves warned! But it's best not to fight fire with fire, and instead to find ways to show newly evolved Pokémon patience and understanding.

When Monferno tried to use Blaze Kick to bust out of Team Rocket's cage, the move sent the Playful Pokémon into a fury. When its Trainer Ash hugged it to show he cared, his support helped Monferno channel its energy into evolving again, into Infernape!

In the Village of Dragons, one of a pair of Zweilous friends evolved into Hydreigon. It was so confused by its Evolution, it went on a rampage. Luckily, Iris and her Pokémon buddy Dragonite were there to calm Hydreigon down.

After Dawn's Pokémon pal Swinub evolved into Piloswine, it refused to listen to its Trainer and only cared about chowing down. But when Team Rocket tried to lure it into a trap with tasty food, Piloswine battled them back, and even evolved again, into Mamoswine!

Anger can sometimes even be the emotion that inspires Evolution. For example, during a battle with the Trainer that had abandoned it long ago, Tepig was flooded with feelings—and then evolved into Pignite and won the match. It sure showed that old Trainer what he was missing!

A Whole Lotta Love

They say love will always find a way— and that certainly applies to Evolution. Don't underestimate the power of a Pokémon in love!

For Mareanie, it was love at first sight when it spotted James of Team Rocket. But its mentor (a fellow Mareanie) had a crush on *it*! What a love triangle! In order to prove its love, the mentor

Mareanie evolved into Toxapex just to be able to poison James—its romantic competition. Dazed and confused from the poison, James insisted Mareanie should be with Toxapex. Mareanie was so hurt by this, it cried. So Toxapex decided to try to win Mareanie back by challenging James to a battle. That proved to be a fool's errand, because James easily defeated the lovesick Pokémon suitor. Mareanie was overjoyed to be reunited with the keeper of its heart, James.

While on its own and on the prowl, Meowth of Team Rocket fell hard for Glameow. But when Meowth finally reunited with Jessie and James, all they wanted to do was capture its beloved Glameow and give it to the Boss. Gutted, Meowth ran away with Glameow. Soon, Team Rocket and Glameow's Trainer caught up with them, and Meowth slashed Fury Swipes to protect its love. But during the battle, gorgeous Glameow evolved into Purugly, and Meowth instantly lost interest. Who said "love is blind"? It certainly wasn't Meowth!

On Chrysanthemum Island, Ash's pal Grovyle fell for Nurse Joy's lovely assistant Meganium. But Grovyle was devastated when it learned Meganium and Grovyle's rival Tropius were a couple. Jealous, Grovyle challenges Tropius to a rematch—until their battle was cut short when Team Rocket swooped in and

stole Meganium and Tropius. To stop the terrible trio, Grovyle evolved into Sceptile, but even in its Evolution, it couldn't seem to blast off the bad guys. However, Meganium and Tropius made such a good team, they were able to defeat Team Rocket themselves—and that allowed Sceptile to see that they were meant to be together. Of course, Ash was there to care for his Pokémon pal to help it through the heartbreak.

To Protect and Defend

"A friend in need is a friend indeed." Pokémon certainly live up to this motto, and are always ready to offer help. Sometimes, their desire to protect their pals is the very emotion that spurs Evolution.

On a ferry to Twinleaf Town, Team Rocket unleashed a group of Tentacruel to poison all the adorable little Pokémon on board. Luckily, Nurse Joy soon arrived and with her helper Happiny. The pink Pokémon was so devoted to healing its cute patients that it evolved into Chansey.

Team Rocket wanted to steal Mt. Molteau's most famous resident, the Legendary Pokémon Moltres. Of course, the mighty Moltres could protect itself, and blasted the trio off with a ferocious Flamethrower. Unfortunately, it also thought Ash and his buddies were bad guys, too. While trying to protect its pals, Fletchinder evolved into terrific Talonflame!

During a festival to honor Zapdos, Team Rocket riled up the Legendary Pokémon, provoking it to cause a terrible lighting storm. Ash and his pals hid out in a cave during the storm, where they met a paramedic who desperately needed to bring special medicine to a patient at the local hospital. Brave Talonflame and Hawlucha tried to distract Zapdos so Ash could sneak out and make the delivery. But when Zapdos knocked Hawlucha down, Noibat evolved into Noivern to save its friend.

WHO CAN HELP POKÉMON EVOLVE?

You don't have to be a Pokémon's Trainer to help it evolve. You don't even have to be a Pokémon Trainer at all! Anyone and everyone can help—the key is to be there for the Pokémon and care about it when it evolves.

When Angie accidentally helped a Lickitung she was watching at her parents' day care evolve into Lickilicky, she hid it in a cave so she wouldn't get in trouble. She was so embarrassed that she had a hand in evolving another Trainer's Pokémon without discussing it with them! She knew it was a big no-no to meddle with another Trainer's Pokémon pal, but she didn't realize it would happen while she was teaching Lickitung Rollout. Meanwhile, Lickilicky kept escaping and scaring the locals of Solaceon Town—they called it the "Scarf Monster." Finally, the Trainer returned to the day care center, and Angie confessed and apologized. But to her surprise, Lickilicky's Trainer was thrilled! Angie had worried herself and the town over nothing.

EEVEE AND ITS EVOLUTIONS

Amazing Eevee is called the Evolution Pokémon. It might be a Normal-type, but there is nothing normal about this unbelievable and unpredictable Pokémon! Due to its sensitive genetic makeup, it will react to its surroundings, the radiation from a variety of rocks, the time of day, and even its Trainer's feelings. Eevee can respond to all those possibilities by changing its shape, size, and even type. As a result, Eevee has an extraordinary eight-branch Evolution.

EEVEE

The Evolution Pokémon

Height: 1'00"   Weight: 14.3 lbs.   Type: Normal

VAPOREON

The Bubble Jet Pokémon

Height: 3'03" Weight: 63.9 lbs.
Type: Water

Water listens to Vaporeon's commands. But not only can the Bubble Jet Pokémon bend water to its will, thanks to its fins and gills, it can live completely under the sea.

Eevee can evolve into Vaporeon with the help of a Water Stone.

JOLTEON

The Lightning Pokémon

Height: 2'07" Weight: 54.0 lbs.
Type: Electric

If you try to pet Jolteon, you're in for a shock! Its spiky needle fur stands on end because of the static electricity. Charged-up Jolteon can blast thunderbolts.

Eevee evolves into Jolteon with the help of a Thunder Stone.

FLAREON

The Flame Pokémon

Height: 2'11" Weight: 55.1 lbs.
Type: Fire

No matter the season, Flareon is always feeling hot. So hot, it will break your thermometer, unless it goes up to a whopping 1,650 degrees Fahrenheit! Luckily, the fluffy fur that covers its body helps it beat the heat by releasing heat into the air.

Eevee evolves into Flareon with the help of a Fire Stone.

ESPEON
The Sun Pokémon

Height: 2'11" Weight: 58.4 lbs.
Type: Psychic

Eevee evolves into Espeon in the sunshine.

The orb on Espeon's head doesn't just add flare, it absorbs strength from the sun's rays. Thanks to the bright light, it is a formidable foe. It seems Espeon's psychic powers stem from its need for self-defense.

UMBREON
The Moonlight Pokémon

Height: 3'03" Weight: 59.5 lbs.
Type: Dark

When Eevee senses the moon's waves, it evolves into Umbreon.

Pokémon fans are over the moon for the Moonlight Pokémon! When it's ready to attack, the golden rings on its body glow. But it does not need the nightlight—Umbreon can battle in pitch-black because its eyes can see even in pure darkness.

LEAFEON
The Verdant Pokémon

Height: 3'03" Weight: 56.2 lbs.
Type: Grass

Eevee can evolve into Leafeon with the help of a Moss Rock.

Leafeon loves to soak up the sunshine. Like a plant, it then uses the power of photosynthesis to create clean air.

GLACEON
The Fresh Snow Pokémon

Height: 2'07" Weight: 57.1 lbs.
Type: Ice

Eevee can evolve into Glaceon with the help of an Ice Rock.

Forget making it rain—Glaceon can make it hail! The Fresh Snow Pokémon really knows how to chill out, and can lower its body temperature even below subzero. To protect itself, it can freeze its fur into needles that shield it from its foes.

SYLVEON

The Intertwining Pokémon

Height: 3'03" Weight: 51.8 lbs.
Type: Fairy

Eevee ca
evolve int
Sylveon with
of love from
Trainer and
ability to perf
one Fairy-ty
move.

Sylveon's streamers are actually feelers that it uses to sense its Trainer's mood. Truth be told, Sylveon is always feeling ready to battle a Dragon-type. It can't resist the fierce fight!

TEAM EEVEE TO THE RESCUE

Near Vertress City in the Unova region, there is a special squad of Eevee and seven of its Evolutions devoted to helping those in need. Virgil, his brother Davy, and his father, Jeff, lead this highly trained and dedicated Pokémon Rescue Squad. So if you find yourself in hot water near the Un League, don't worry—Eevee, Jolteon, Espeon, Flareon, Jolteon, Leafeon Glaceon, and Vaporeon will be there to save the day!

THE MYSTERIOUS EVOLUTION OF COSMOG

Cosmog might only be eight inches tall, but it holds one of the biggest mysteries of the Pokémon world. Scientists have yet to uncover Cosmog's origins. It possesses the power of teleportation and can escape danger in a flash. Some think the gaseous Pokémon it is not even of this world. It is so light, it simply goes anywhere the wind takes it.

COSMOG
The Nebula Pokémon

Height: 0'08"   Weight: 0.2 lbs.   Type: Psychic

COSMOEM

When Cosmog evolves into Cosmoem, it gains over one ton of weight and is encased in a solid golden shell. Despite its heft, Cosmoem also floats in midair. This Pokémon is so strong and stunning, an ancient ruler of the Alola region built a shrine in its honor and nicknamed the Pokémon the "cocoon of the stars."

COSMOEM
The Protostar Pokémon

Height: 0'04"
Weight: 2204.4 lbs.
Type: Psychic

LUNALA
The Moone Pokémon

Height: 13'01"
Weight: 264.6 lbs.
Type: Psychic/Ghost

LUNALA

Cosmoem actually has a branched Evolution. Under different conditions, Cosmoem could evolve into another Legendary Pokémon, Lunala, the Moone Pokémon.

SOLGALEO

Cosmoem evolved into the Legendary Pokémon Solgaleo at the Altar of the Sunne in a special ceremony! First, the Alola region's Island Guardians—Tapu Bulu, Tapu Fini, Tapu Koko, and Tapu Lele—gathered at the shrine. Together, they covered the area in all four Terrain Moves. Then they each floated atop a pedestal and focused their energy. A blue glow filled the carvings of the altar and shot up the central pillar. The stone unlocked, revealing a glowing golden sphere. From the sphere, a rainbow light landed on Cosmoem and created an orb around it. Bathed in this light, Cosmoem evolved into the awesome Sunne Pokémon Solgaleo. That gave it the power to travel through an Ultra Wormhole into the world of the Ultra Beasts.

SOLGALEO
The Sunne Pokémon

Height: 11'02"
Weight: 507.1 lbs.
Type: Psychic/
Steel

Cosmog

Cosmoem

Solgaleo

Lunala

MARVELOUS MEGA EVOLUTION

Mega Evolution is an Evolution Forme that is too powerful to be permanent. Pokémon that Mega Evolve can only do so during battle. It is a temporary boost that increases their power to such great heights that it makes a Pokémon nearly unstoppable!

Only a select group of Pokémon possess the ability to Mega Evolve, and even then, it's not a simple process. First and foremost, a Trainer must develop a deep bond with their Pokémon pal. They must truly understand and rely on each other—complete trust is the foundation of Mega Evolution. Trainers go to great lengths in order to achieve this connection. The roller-skating Gym Leader of Shalour City, Korrina, vowed to win one hundred battles in a row with her super-skillful Lucario before even attempting to have it Mega Evolve for the first time.

In addition to their alliance, a Trainer must also posses a rare Key Stone and an even rarer Mega Stone for Mega Evolution.

THE KEY IN KEY STONE

The Key Stone gives a Trainer and their Pokémon pal the ability to communicate without saying a word. They can read each other's minds and see things through each other's eyes. Since Pokémon who can Mega Evolve are even more desirable to Pokémon Poachers and Hunters, the Key Stone can also play a very important role as a tracking device. Thanks to the Key Stone, a Trainer can always tell exactly where their Pokémon is, no matter how far it travels.

The Key Stone's least important (but most fabulous!) purpose is fashion. The shiny stone orb is worn by the Trainer as part of their outfit—added to a glove, belt, bracelet, or any accessory.

THE MAGNIFICENT MEGA STONE

Unlike the Key Stone, Mega Stones are Pokémon-specific. For example, Lucario requires the Mega Stone Lucarionite, Garchomp needs Garchompite, Sharpedo will use Sharpedonite, and so on.

A dedicated Trainer must quest for the proper Mega Stone. However, even if a Trainer finds the correct Mega Stone and it's within their grasp, they still might not be able to get their hands on it. A Mega Stone can only be handled by someone who is prepared to wield its precious power.

These treasured Mega Stones are often found in mountainous regions of Kalos. A popular destination for Trainers seeking their Mega Stone is Geosenge Town. Hidden deep within a cave there, Korrina located Lucarionite.

MEGA STARS OF MEGA EVOLUTION

Diantha

The Champion of Kalos, Diantha, is the strongest Trainer in all of Kalos, and one of the region's famous movie stars. In addition to her big-screen performances, she loves to take the stage on the battlefield. She tours the region showing off her skills in exhibition battles with her showstopping, Mega Evolving Gardevoir.

Mabel

If a Trainer is seeking advice on Mega Evolution, they should visit a particular resident of Pomace Mountain: Mabel. Wise old Mabel knows just how to help a young Trainer. Along with her Pokémon partner, a Mega Evolving Mawile, Mabel can whip any dedicated Trainer and their Pokémon pal into shape, but it will take hard work!

Gurkinn

Gurkinn is a Mega Evolution expert and descendent of the first Trainer to help a Pokémon Mega Evolve. To honor the family history, he and his granddaughter Korrina focus their training on their Pokémon friends Lucario.

SACRED SHALOUR CITY

According to Legend, the first known Mega Evolution happened in Shalour City. An ancestor of Korrina, the Gym Leader of Shalour City, is thought to have arrived on the island with his Pokémon Lucario. Right on the spot where the Tower of Mastery now stands, it is said that he found two unique stones that spawned the first Mega Evolution. Korrina and her grandfather Gurkinn see it as their family duty to safeguard this sacred site and protect the importance of Mega Evolution.

MEGA EVOLVING POKÉMON INDEX

Pokémon		Mega Stone			Mega Evolved
Abomasnow	✛	Abomasite			Mega Abomasnow
Absol	✛	Absolite			Mega Absol
Aerodactyl	✛	Aerodactylite			Mega Aerodactyl
Aggron	✛	Aggronite			Mega Aggron
Alakazam	✛	Alakazite			Mega Alakazam
Altaria	✛	Altarianite			Mega Altaria
Ampharos	✛	Ampharosite			Mega Ampharos
Audino	✛	Audinite			Mega Audino
Banette	✛	Banettite			Mega Banette
Beedrill	✛	Beedrillite			Mega Beedrill
Blastoise	✛	Blastoisinite			Mega Blastoise
Blaziken	✛	Blazikenite			Mega Blaziken
Camerupt	✛	Cameruptite			Mega Camerupt
Charizard	✛	Charizardite X			Mega Charizard X
Charizard	✛	Charizardite Y			Mega Charizard Y
Diancie	✛	Diancite			Mega Diancie
Gallade	✛	Galladite			Mega Gallade
Garchomp	✛	Garchompite			Mega Garchomp
Gardevoir	✛	Gardevoirite			Mega Gardevoir
Gengar	✛	Gengarite			Mega Gengar
Glalie	✛	Glalitite			Mega Glalie
Gyarados	✛	Gyaradosite			Mega Gyarados
Heracross	✛	Heracronite			Mega Heracross

Pokémon		Mega Stone		Mega Evolved
Houndoom	✚	Houndoominite	⊟	Mega Houndoom
Kangaskhan	✚	Kangaskhanite	⊟	Mega Kangaskhan
Latias	✚	Latiasite	⊟	Mega Latias
Latios	✚	Latiosite	⊟	Mega Latios
Lopunny	✚	Lopunnite	⊟	Mega Lopunny
Lucario	✚	Lucarionite	⊟	Mega Lucario
Manectric	✚	Manectite	⊟	Mega Manectric
Mawile	✚	Mawilite	⊟	Mega Mawile
Medicham	✚	Medichamite	⊟	Mega Medicham
Metagross	✚	Metagrossite	⊟	Mega Metagross
Mewtwo	✚	Mewtwonite X	⊟	Mega Mewtwo X
Mewtwo	✚	Mewtwonite Y	⊟	Mega Mewtwo Y
Pidgeot	✚	Pidgeotite	⊟	Mega Pidgeot
Pinsir	✚	Pinsirite	⊟	Mega Pinsir
Sableye	✚	Sablenite	⊟	Mega Sableye
Salamence	✚	Salamencite	⊟	Mega Salamence
Sceptile	✚	Sceptilite	⊟	Mega Sceptile
Scizor	✚	Scizorite	⊟	Mega Scizor
Sharpedo	✚	Sharpedonite	⊟	Mega Sharpedo
Slowbro	✚	Slowbronite	⊟	Mega Slowbro
Steelix	✚	Steelixite	⊟	Mega Steelix
Swampert	✚	Swampertite	⊟	Mega Swampert
Tyranitar	✚	Tyaranitarite	⊟	Mega Tyranitar
Venusaur	✚	Venusaurite	⊟	Mega Venusaur

I CHOOSE YOU!

Cue the confetti, because if you have read all the way through to this last page, you can consider yourself a Pokémon Evolution expert! Since you are an excellent reader, you must be the kind of dedicated person who makes a great Trainer. You certainly have what it takes to help your Pokémon pals evolve and even Mega Evolve.

And if it piques your interest, there is plenty more out there to learn about Pokémon.

Happy reading!